PEOPLE IN GLASS HOUSES

By

Darren Rapier

PEOPLE IN GLASS HOUSES was first presented by DOOM
Productions at The Brockley Jack Theatre, Brockley, on 6th January
1998, with the following cast:

TINA (China)....................................Shelly Atkinson
AMY (America)...........................Francesca Compton
JAN (Japan)...Laura Crowe
URSULA (Russia)...........................Milenka Marosh
BRIAN (Britain).............................Lorne Thomson
RICHARD (Germany)...........................Jon Whiting

Directed by Nick Pilton
Designed by Megan Huish

ISBN 978-0-9556798-0-3

First Published 2007
www.darrenrapier.co.uk

For performance rights of this play please contact:

Andrew Mann Ltd.,
1 Old Compton Street,
London, W1D 5JA
Tel: 020 7734 4751
Fax: 020 7287 9264
info@manscript.co.uk

'Those who do not remember the past are condemned to repeat it.'

George Santayana

<u>SET</u>

The action all takes place in a Glasshouse, erected on the roof of a large office block. The play is set several years in the future, when land is scarce and extremely valuable. There should be subtle hints that the plots of land inside the Glasshouse represent the World map of the Northern hemisphere. This is because the underlying plot predominantly follows the history of the world, through the eyes of America, Britain & France, Germany, Russia, China and Japan, between 1918 and 1941.

PEOPLE IN GLASS HOUSES
by
Darren Rapier

Scene One: The Glasshouse: Mid Morning.

The Glasshouse is situated on the roof of a large building.   There is a door Down Stage Left - the only way in and out.   The floor is divided into five plots, like an allotment, but these are unequal in size.   There is a narrow path DS crossing left to right and a small stream separating plots 001(SR) and 002.   The Glasshouse is in total disarray.   There are pots and plants everywhere, some of the panes of glass are broken.   A couple of deck chairs lie scattered, along with an upturned table and a few garden ornaments.   On plot 004 (the fourth from SR and similar in size to 005) a gnome, resembling Leon Trotsky, has been discarded.   It is obvious there has been a fight between the occupants of the Glasshouse.   From the damage it is clear this mainly took place in the middle area (plots 002 and 003), borders are smudged and plastic fences broken.

RICHARD walks into the Glasshouse and looks around, he sneezes.   He sighs.   It is the first time he has seen the Glasshouse and he has inherited this small plot from his uncle.   Producing a piece of paper from his pocket, he compares the plan he has to the floor space and works out where his plot should be.   It is third from the door, (003) larger than plot 002 but smaller than 004 and 005.   He begins to clear his plot, throwing the rubbish into an old wheel barrow.

Enter URSULA, she is also a new tenant.   She has arrived early, in her dungarees, ready to sort out her plot.   She stops in her tracks when she sees RICHARD.   He turns.

URSULA: William?

- 5 -

RICHARD: No, thank goodness.

URSULA: Oh. Do you know where I might find him?

RICHARD: Holland.

URSULA: Oh. (*Smiles*).

> *URSULA takes a packet of seeds from her pocket and throws them onto the ground of her plot (004, second from left). Seeing this RICHARD takes out his piece of paper and compares it to URSULA's plot. He smiles and holds out his hand in greeting.*

RICHARD: Ah, you must be Ursula?

URSULA: (*Surprised*). Yes. (*She wipes her hand on her dungarees and shakes RICHARD's*).

RICHARD: (*Producing a note book from his pocket*). I believe you came to a little arrangement with Bill.

> *URSULA looks at him, unsure of what to say.*

RICHARD: To the tune of four tools, a third of your plot, half of your plants?

> *URSULA smiles at him, uneasily.*

RICHARD: Oh, and sixty thousand to cover expenses.

> *Pause as URSULA tries to restrain herself form hitting RICHARD.*

RICHARD: Well?

URSULA: But Bill isn't here, besides I never met him, there's nothing in writing.

RICHARD: A deal's a deal. I'm in charge of his plot now. So cough up. (*He holds out his hand*).

URSULA begrudgingly hands over several packets of seeds, four small hand tools and the money. RICHARD smiles.   URSULA glares at him then returns to tidying her plot.
RICHARD moves over to URSULA's plot, he watches her but she ignores him. He starts marking the ground with his foot, as if bored, scuffing the dirt along a line.

RICHARD: Look I'm sorry, but that's the way it is, heaven knows it's hard enough to get hold of a decent sized bit of land these days. The bank's made me the custodian of Bill's plot and I have to show them I can look after it... it's nothing personal.

URSULA remains silent.

RICHARD: We may as well try to get on at least... *(Pause)* Who rents your plot then? I mean, how did you manage to become custodian? These things are like gold dust.

URSULA still remains silent. RICHARD looks down at the line he has drawn.

RICHARD: *(Gloating, fed up with trying to be polite)* I'd say that's about a third, wouldn't you?

URSULA glares. RICHARD smiles and then continues his tidying. URSULA only has one tool left, a small ice pick. She starts to tear out all the flowers and anything else decorative.

URSULA: A few meters of earth, the potential to grow anything you want and what do I have: The laughing gnome. *(She holds up the gnome and throws him onto the rubbish pile she has made).*

AMY enters, she has a bag full of new tools, seeds, plants, a picnic and a new chair. She stops at the pile of rubbish and picks up the gnome.

AMY: Oh, someone's thrown away little Leon by mistake.

URSULA and RICHARD turn to look at her.

AMY: Hi there.

URSULA: Drop dead. (*She returns to her sorting*).

AMY: Charming. (*She looks at the gnome*). Well, never mind Leon, you come and live with me.

AMY moves towards her plot, (001 - the biggest plot). RICHARD walks over to meet her, he holds out his hand, she simply looks at him. RICHARD smiles nervously and withdraws the gesture.

AMY: You must be Richard?

RICHARD: Yes.

AMY: Hmmm.

AMY simply looks at the mess in the middle plot. She places her chair on the ground and sits down. RICHARD waits for a while to see if any conversation will spark up. He begins to feel invisible and returns to his plot.

The three of them occupy themselves for a few moments. AMY starts to take out her picnic, after putting the gnome down safely. RICHARD continues to mark out the edges of his plot, working out how big it is. URSULA continues throwing everything off her plot into the pile of rubbish.

URSULA: I can see there's going to be a big bonfire tonight.

AMY: (*Without looking over at her*). Bonfires are forbidden.

URSULA: Do you think I'm paying to dump this lot? There's going to be some changes on this plot: No more ponsing around with pretty flowers, perfect lawns and gnomes. If you've got land, use it, or get off it and make way for someone who will.

AMY: *(Still not looking at her).* You won't make any friends with that attitude.

URSULA: I don't need friends like you. This earth isn't here for a few to gloat over, it's here for the benefit of all. Perhaps if we'd realised that earlier there wouldn't be thousands of empty offices, that will never be filled, congested roads spiralling into nowhere. Perhaps there would be clean air, fresh water, soft earth under foot, that doesn't belong to anyone, but belongs to everyone.

RICHARD: *(Dismissively)* We have clean air.

URSULA: We have filtered air.

RICHARD: Look I don't know what your complaining about, you've got your plot. People would die to have that opportunity, half of them think these Glasshouses only exist in stories.

URSULA: A few meters of earth, in a landscape of concrete.

AMY: If you don't like it why don't you go back down inside? I'm sure your distillery can find someone else to look after the plot for them.   It's extremely valuable.

URSULA: Every inch of earth is valuable. If we hadn't spent years eroding it, inch by precious inch, producing plants, vegetables - even animals - that have never seen a green field...

RICHARD: Green fields are a thing of the past: Like Gas lighting;
            horse drawn carriages and houses with gardens. They
            represent a waste of useful space.

URSULA: Then why is that patch of soil so important to you?

RICHARD: Luckily, our companies had the foresight to see that one
            day land would be fashionable again. We may consider
            ourselves lucky to control a small, yet valuable piece of
            antiquity.

URSULA: Antiquity?

RICHARD: When it was in abundance people abused it, built on it,
            destroyed it, as with all antiques. Now it's left to the
            connoisseur, to respect, admire, boast about and, if he
            wishes, misuse.

AMY: Hear, hear. Would you like a tea cake?

*Off stage a large clock strikes eleven. All stop dead to listen to it.
RICHARD looks at his watch.*

AMY: Oh dear, and I was just getting to like you.

*BRIAN marches in, followed by JAN and TINA. JAN and TINA
stop just inside the door. There is obviously some resentment
towards TINA on JAN's part..
JAN is quietly confident, TINA a little nervous.
BRIAN walks to the upturned table and places it upright.
Suddenly he notices the wheel barrow full of RICHARD's rubbish.
 He walks over to it and tips it up, taking the barrow to his own
plot (002).*

BRIAN: You're not using that.

He puts a brief case onto the table and opens it, taking out a piece of paper. He clears his throat.

BRIAN: After much discussion, myself and my colleagues have reached the following decisions about the future of plot number 003.

AMY walks over and joins BRIAN at the table.

BRIAN: We have decided that the blame for damage, particularly to plot 002, lies solely with the current owner of 003.

RICHARD: But.......

BRIAN: Over the last few days we have drawn up our demands for compensation and shall instruct our insurance companies within the week.

RICHARD is about to interrupt but AMY presses her finger to her lips, indicating it would not be a good idea.

BRIAN: We feel these demands are in the interest of all.

AMY: I'd just like to say, these were drawn up for the sake of peace and not futile revenge.

BRIAN: Quite. Firstly I will read out a short statement that we will be asking you to sign: "The Allied and Associated Custodians affirm, and the Current Custodian of plot 003 accepts, the responsibility for causing all the loss and damage, to which the Allied Associated Custodians and their plots have been subjected, as a consequence of the conflict imposed upon them by the aggression of the Current Custodian of plot 003".

RICHARD is speechless for a moment.

RICHARD: *(Politely)* I can understand your resentment... and I can only apologise for my uncle's behaviour - a flagrant misuse of his privileges - but I can hardly...

BRIAN: Your uncle threatened the very fabric of our lives in this Glasshouse, he could have destroyed everything.

RICHARD: But a guilt clause...

JAN: Would you rather your bank lost it's share in the house altogether?

RICHARD: Well no but... I can't sign for something I had no part in.

BRIAN: You are guilty by association. How are we to know you didn't encourage him in his bid to take over?

RICHARD: We've re-structured the bank since then...

BRIAN: Surely you would have benefited if he had succeeded?

RICHARD: That's not the point...

BRIAN: Look I'm sorry, but I'm afraid it is the point: That's the way it is, heaven knows it's hard enough to get hold of a decent sized bit of land these days.

URSULA grins. RICHARD grits his teeth.

BRIAN: I'll let you read the rest, then we can all sign it tomorrow. There's a copy here for everyone. *(Brian hands out copies).*

Snatching his copy RICHARD sighs and leaves the Glasshouse abruptly.

BRIAN: Well that's got that over with. Pub anyone?

AMY and JAN nod in acceptance and leave with BRIAN.
URSULA and TINA stand for a moment and then URSULA returns
to her plot.   TINA watches.   There is pause before...

TINA: Looks like I was quite lucky in some ways.   *(Referring to*
                 the damage on her plot).

URSULA: You're telling me.

TINA: What was it like?

URSULA is slightly puzzled by this and turns to face TINA.

URSULA: What?

TINA: 'The Great Fight'.

URSULA: You weren't here?

TINA: No, my nephew had the plot then.   Lucky little devil.

URSULA: How old is he?

TINA: Two.

URSULA: Two!   Your company let a two year old run your plot?

TINA: Yea.

URSULA: That is totally irresponsible, he could have ruined it.

TINA: I think they thought he'd be a push over.   All this "one
                 custodian per plot", you know, the managers saw
                 themselves up here with their mistresses when it was
                 quiet, that sort of thing.   I think the pressure got too much
                 for him in the end: He wanted slides, sandpits -

completely out of the question of course. Yes, tantrums, the lot - he had to resign. Terrible two's eh?

URSULA thinks for a moment.

URSULA: So, how comes you're running the plot?

TINA: I was the only one available at the time, between you and me, the company's going through a bit of a bad patch at the moment: Lot of back stabbing. They wanted someone they could trust. I'll only be here for a while.

URSULA: Better make the most of it then.

TINA: Eh?

URSULA: While you're up here they don't know what's going on. It's up to you what happens.

TINA: Yea, but you don't know how hard it is. I can't move a blade of grass without permission, I have to take photographs, report daily to the board......

URSULA: I know how hard it is. But it can change. All these plots used to be inheritance only. Nicholas grew fruit, played croquet, did what he liked and answered to no one. Half of us workers at the distillery didn't even know our company owned a plot. Then, after the fight - when it was nearly too late -, we asked: Why can't everyone benefit, why can't we all have fresh fruit? We nearly lost our plot because of a fight involving others. I campaigned hard. I offered peace, fruit and veg and a plot that benefited all. History would never have forgiven me if I hadn't seized power then. I may have lost some things on the way, but mark my words I'll get them back.

Scene Two: The Glasshouse: Later The Same Day.

*URSULA's plot is cleared of all rubbish and the pile has gone.
TINA and URSULA have also gone and AMY, BRIAN and JAN sit
talking on AMY's plot.   They all have drinks but are not drunk.*

BRIAN: Now come on Amy, you've got to sign.

AMY: I'd rather have the cash that's all, it doesn't affect you.   I
            can run my plot as I see fit, I don't want any part of your
            silly squabbles.

BRIAN: You won't have a plot if it happens again, the water that
            separates us is only one step away.   If Richard decides to
            go the same way as Bill did, don't think he'll stop here.

AMY: I'm not fighting again, it's as simple as that, and your
            insurance claim will only aggravate the situation.

BRIAN: But I owe it to my company, Francis is positively
            seething, she feels the application is far too lenient.

AMY: I'm sorry.

JAN: I think Richard is getting exactly what he deserves.

BRIAN: Thank you Jan.

JAN: However, I can't say that I'm exactly happy with the
            agreement either.

        BRIAN sighs.

JAN: I helped as much as possible to stop the conflict, even
            though I haven't got a plot in here.   I had hoped that the

effort on my part would be somehow repaid, with a token gesture - not much - just a small piece of the end plot.

BRIAN: Jan, there's no way...

JAN: I don't dislike my own small piece of land, there's a lot to be said for an ornamental plot in the middle of a pond, but I feel it's about time I was given control of plot 005. So I can manage it as it should be managed.

BRIAN: But it's up to the custodian to manage it as they see fit, it's in the rules.

JAN: With control of that plot I could easily make it fifty times better, she's got no idea what she's doing. I thought that by helping I'd be allowed to move in here, instead it seems the only people who'll really gain are you and Amy.

BRIAN: My plot was virtually destroyed.

JAN: Would you rather be out in the pond?

BRIAN: There is far more at stake here than personal gain. For a start we have three new custodians running plots. Tina won't be around long but Richard and Ursula are here to stay.

AMY: I wouldn't be so sure of that, I can see Ursula being a problem.

JAN: I agree, she's got some weird ideas.

BRIAN: Fine well let's start there. We'll write to her distillery and tell them we're not happy with their choice of custodian.

JAN: Why not write to the owner of the Glasshouse as well?

AMY: The owner?   But what if he comes down and sees what
                we've done?

JAN: He's never come down since I've been here.

BRIAN: He can't get rid of us, the leases have got years to run yet.

AMY: But still...

BRIAN: We'll think about it.   Now what about Richard?

JAN: Well, as he's related to William, we could just bar him.

AMY: We're not legally allowed to do that.

JAN: Then what do you suggest?

AMY: Leave it to me, I have a few 'influential' friends.

       They clink glasses.

BRIAN: Good.   Now let's move on.

JAN: Well, firstly I need somewhere in here for my caterpillars.

AMY: What?

JAN: It's far too cold outside for them.   I only need a little bit
                of space.   How about Tina's plot?

BRIAN: How many times do I have to tell you...

JAN: Just a foot or so.   They're delicate creatures.

BRIAN: *(Unable to take any more)*   I'll see what I can do.

JAN: Thank you. Oh, and Amy, did you still want those dresses?

AMY: Yes definitely.

JAN: Good, things are a bit quiet at the moment.

BRIAN: Can we get on with the meeting?

JAN: Sorry.

BRIAN: Now the pond.

JAN: Yes.

BRIAN: I think we're all agreed that Richard should not be allowed to have any fish at all.

JAN: Agreed.

AMY: There's only enough space for thirteen fish anyway.

BRIAN: That's right. So, if Amy and I have Five each, you can have the other three.

JAN: How comes I only get three? I'm the nearest one to the pond, I'm in it.

BRIAN: We don't want to stretch your finances.

JAN: My finances are fine. Why can't you have three? You're the one who's lost so much business.

AMY: We have to remain the same, showing unity.

JAN: Have four each then: That way they'll have a bit more space.

BRIAN: Jan, it's already decided!

JAN stands.

JAN: I helped you and this is the thanks I get?

BRIAN: Look, I'll try and sort something out with Tina.

JAN: You'd better!

JAN storms out, leaving AMY and BRIAN wondering if the Glasshouse will ever be the same again.

Scene Three: The Glasshouse: The following day.

URSULA is working on her plot, digging frantically.
RICHARD enters, he sits down, trying to relax.   URSULA's work
becomes even more frantic.

RICHARD: What is the matter with you?

URSULA: What?

RICHARD: What's the matter with you?   I came in here to relax.

URSULA: Oh.

RICHARD: Can't you do that some other time?

URSULA: Can't you relax some other time?

RICHARD: No.

URSULA: Fine.   *(Continues).*

RICHARD: Look please, I have a very important meeting to attend
               this evening.

URSULA: So do I.

RICHARD: I would like to make the most of my time here.

URSULA: So would I.

RICHARD: I may not even be here tomorrow.

URSULA: Snap.

RICHARD: *(Surprised)*   What?

URSULA: I have a meeting with the board this evening, to decide whether 'I deserve to run the plot'.

RICHARD: I'm sorry I didn't know.

URSULA: And you?

RICHARD: Oh, there's been a complaint about me being up here, from one of our 'influential' customers.   It was so much easier when Inheritance meant that all these endless discussions, about who has the right to do what, didn't exist.

URSULA: Autocracy is no substitute for democracy.

RICHARD: So you'd rather have all these 'debates' and 'discussions', even if it means inevitably you get the boot?

URSULA: If we're unable to reason with each other, surely we're no better than animals?

RICHARD: Are you sure you can say we are?

URSULA: Some of us.

RICHARD laughs.

RICHARD: They all want me out. Half of them want to grow vegetables and be self sufficient, the other half want it for exclusive leisure use. It's just that usually they're too afraid to say anything, don't want to rock the boat. You just need one person to say what they really think and it sets the others off, nodding like a convoy of little turds drifting down the sewer.

Pause. URSULA looks at him for a moment before...

URSULA: We've got more in common than you think.

RICHARD: How do you work that out?

URSULA: Why do you think things are suddenly going wrong for
               us?   How is it we can reach a point in our respective
               companies, without a hitch, only to find that now our
               position is being subverted?   It's because we are here.
               Because we've arrived at the top table.

RICHARD: What are you going on about?

URSULA: Don't you see?   They want to get rid of us *(indicating
               Amy and Brian's plots).*

RICHARD: Why?

URSULA: Because we represent a threat to them.

RICHARD: Oh come on, I'm not even allowed to use the bloody
               wheel barrow.

URSULA: I'll guarantee they're behind it.

RICHARD: You have a serious paranoia problem.   They're bleeding
               me dry and loving every minute of it, they don't need to
               go behind my back to humiliate me.

URSULA: I'm just saying that perhaps together we could...

RICHARD: Join you?   I'd rather join Brian and Amy, at least I
               wouldn't be wasting my time digging for potatoes when I
               can buy them at the supermarket.   *(He laughs).*

        URSULA scowls at him.

URSULA: So you think you can take them on, on your own?

RICHARD: *(Smiling)* I don't need to take them on.   I'll join them - against you.

Scene Four: The Glasshouse: Later that evening.

The Glasshouse is in darkness.   In the distance we can hear the voices of AMY, JAN and BRIAN.   They are gradually getting louder.

AMY (Off):   I think it's disgraceful.

BRIAN (Off):   Apparently she tore the letter up there and then, and declared the meeting closed.

AMY (Off):   Still in her dungarees I'll bet.

JAN (Off):   I didn't think she had it in her.

AMY (Off):   Believe me we've got a struggle on there.

BRIAN (Off):   Everything seemed so promising as well.

The lights of the Glasshouse are turned on.   BRIAN, AMY and JAN enter.

AMY: I would have been prepared to offer her drinks on my plot.   Am I not considered to be the most sociable custodian?

BRIAN and JAN nod.

AMY (Cont.):   My plot is a safe haven for any living creature, it is free to all who wish to visit.   Any small animal or insect may find safe retreat.   "Those huddled masses yearning to breath free", may do so here. *(She walks over to her plot and as she gets there sees an ant).* Damn ants! *(She steps on it).*

JAN: Erm, may I join you Amy, it's a little cold out and, well you know how small my plot is.

BRIAN walks over to RICHARD's plot and marks back his boarder, leaving a gap between his own plot and RICHARD's, as...

AMY: Of course Jan, no need to ask.

BRIAN: Has anyone managed to get anything out of the owner?

AMY: I phoned again today and left a message, but he never gets back to you.

BRIAN walks onto RICHARD's plot, he marks out a wide boarder either side as he speaks, effectively forming two corridors (the one on URSULA's side taking up the land RICHARD had taken and a bit more).

BRIAN: His endorsement would be invaluable, pull everyone in to line.

JAN: As long as he was on our side.

BRIAN: What?

JAN: As long as he didn't disagree with us.

BRIAN: Not at all. As long as what he says is right and just, that's the issue here. Naturally it just so happens that our ethical standpoint is the right one, he'd be able to see that.

He joins AMY and JAN for a drink.
URSULA enters. The other three fall into an uneasy silence.

URSULA: Thought I might find you here. *(Pause).* I'm surprised you haven't contaminated my soil.

AMY: *(Sarcastically)* We hadn't thought of that.

BRIAN and JAN look at each other.

BRIAN: *(Uneasily to Ursula)* We just felt that you might be making a wrong decision on your plot, that's all. Before you know it the whole structure of the Glasshouse could be changed.

URSULA: I hope it is.

JAN: There's no need to be...

URSULA: I plan to get to a stage where every month the names, of all the employees, are put into a hat and every day a different person is allowed on the plot.

BRIAN: I'm sorry but you can't just...

AMY: *(Astonished and horrified)* A different person every day? We won't be able to form bridge clubs, or leave the Monopoly board set up over night.

URSULA: That's OK there won't be time for games. Besides, when everyone sees that they can share in the running of a plot, I'm sure you'll be the first to be voted out.

AMY drinks down her drink quickly.

BRIAN: Look, Ursula let's forget our little misunderstandings...

URSULA: You should have thought of that before sending the letter.

BRIAN: ...   Before that ridiculous fight everything was fine, we all helped each other. What's the point of growing all this food? We should be enjoying our time here. I've lost some of my best customers, simply because I've been spending too much time in here trying to sort out arguments. Now I don't want that to happen again. I run a grocery business, I'm sure that I could offer you a good price on what ever you want.

URSULA: Listen to you. Half an hour ago you would gladly have got rid of me, now you offer me token friendship. No thanks. I didn't realise that you were all so afraid of change.

AMY: We've spoken to the owner.

URSULA: He doesn't care about you, he's probably forgotten all about this place.

AMY: You'll see when he comes down to throw you out.

URSULA: Can't you see that here, there is only us. Still, if you think by phoning and writing you can make him listen, you keep on. As far as I'm concerned he doesn't exist. But if the belief, that he will swoop down here and take me away, keeps you happy that's fine by me. Trouble is, that hope of salvation clouds your view of what's really going on, it's like opium. In the mean time I think I'll live my life in the real world.

She turns to face her plot and sees the gap that has been marked between her and RICHARD.

URSULA: What's this?

JAN: It's a sort of buffer zone.

URSULA: A what?

JAN: It's for your own protection.

URSULA: How dare you...

BRIAN: Before you start ranting and raving, it was decided that we'd put in two corridors to protect the plots either side of Richard's, just in case he started...

URSULA: But you've taken some of my land!

JAN: And Richard's.

AMY: Don't worry, it's neutral ground, no-one's allowed to use it.

URSULA: *(Sarcastically)* Oh, well that makes it all right then doesn't it?

BRIAN: I don't think you appreciate what went on here...

URSULA: And I don't think you appreciate that this is my land! Now I can't be bothered to argue over the finer details but I'm coming back with a copy of the deeds.

URSULA storms out, bumping into RICHARD on her way.

RICHARD: What's up with her?

JAN: Oh she's annoyed at the fact that we've bothered to consider other people, in our plans for the future.

RICHARD: What?

BRIAN: Of course there's nothing she can do, the deeds have already been changed - the new borders decided.

BRIAN returns to his own plot, busying himself to avoid eye contact with RICHARD.

RICHARD: New... ? *(He sees the 'corridor' on either side of his plot).*

He turns to look at the others, but like BRIAN they avoid his gaze. RICHARD takes a breath and grits his teeth to hide his anger.

AMY: *(To Richard, without looking).* How are things at the bank?

RICHARD: Oh fine, fine.

AMY looks up, this is not the answer she had been expecting.

AMY: No... problems?

RICHARD: Heavens no. What makes you think I'd have any problems?

AMY: I just thought...

RICHARD: Oh, lucky you're here though.

AMY looks slightly worried that her plan to get rid of RICHARD has backfired. The others turn to see what he is about to say, with trepidation. RICHARD reaches into his pocket, looking at AMY. He pulls out an envelope and holds it abruptly towards her. AMY flinches, as for one moment she thinks it is going to be a gun.

RICHARD: You did say cash?

AMY sheepishly takes the envelope, much to the disgust of Brian.

RICHARD: It's all there, you can count it, if you like.

BRIAN: You do realise it doesn't change our position, as far as you are concerned.

RICHARD: Naturally.

JAN: We really want to put this whole awful business behind us: Make a fresh start.

RICHARD: I'd be happy to settle things - if you didn't want to go through with the claim.

BRIAN: Out of the question.

RICHARD: Well, if your mind's made up...

BRIAN: I posted the form this morning.

RICHARD: Then that's fine.

BRIAN: Fine.

Pause.

RICHARD: Anyone fancy a drink?

AMY is about to accept, when she sees BRIAN's look of contempt.

BRIAN: We'd rather not.

RICHARD: How did the erm..., I mean did you?...   Ursula?

BRIAN: How did you know about...

AMY: She's still here isn't she?

RICHARD: Oh, I see. *(Pause)* Would you like me to have a word at the bank, see if there's anything I can...

BRIAN: We don't need your help, thank you.

RICHARD: Right, of course.   Still can't interest anyone in that drink
            then?

Silence.
RICHARD bows politely and exits.

BRIAN: *(To Amy, sharply)* I thought you said you had 'influential'
            friends?

AMY: I do. Mr. Wolf is one of their best customers, he assured
            me Richard would be out within an hour of his visit.

JAN: It seems our new neighbours are here to stay.

AMY: I don't understand, he's had chairmen crying at that bank.

BRIAN: And yet a mere 'manager' can ignore him?

AMY: No, I...   They re-decorated the entire foyer because he
            mentioned he disliked the colour, they worship the man.

JAN: Perhaps this Mr. Wolf decided he liked Richard more
            than you Amy?

AMY: We go back a long way...

JAN: Why should you worry anyway?   You've got your
            money.

BRIAN: Jan please, there's no point in us falling out with each
            other...

JAN: How can you be so stupid, she's got what she wanted, she
            always does.

BRIAN: I really don't think this is the time, we've got to stick
            together...

AMY: No, if Jan's got something to say...

JAN: Oh forget it.

AMY: No, come on Jan.

BRIAN: I will not stand for this bickering amongst ourselves!   We
                must stick together...

JAN: OK then, let's see how we can get rid of Tina...

BRIAN: I really don't think Tina's a problem...

AMY: Or Richard come to that.

BRIAN: *(Disbelief)*   What?

AMY: Well, I mean, he's related to Bill - so what?

BRIAN: So what?

AMY: It's Ursula we should be worried about.

BRIAN: But we've tried...

AMY: She's the one that threatens the whole ethos of the
                Glasshouse.   If we let her get away with this proletarian
                equality bullshit the party's over, believe me.

JAN: And what do you suggest we do, shoot her?

AMY: If it comes to it.

JAN: But get someone else to pull the trigger, right?

AMY: I can fight my own battles, thank you very much.

BRIAN: No-one will be fighting any battles! Haven't you learnt anything from what's happened? Nothing can be achieved by violence. That's why we have to stick to the rules, that's why we have rules - otherwise it's just survival of the fittest.

JAN: Perhaps that's as it should be.

BRIAN: Let's just all calm down! We may well have to live with things as they are for a while, we've just got to accept that. We're going to have to make an effort at getting along, that's all.

TINA appears at the doorway.

TINA: *(Jolly)* Hello everyone.

JAN: Get lost!

Scene Five: The Glasshouse: Two days later, mid day.

URSULA is fixing a video camera up in one corner of her plot, it has a sticker saying 'KGB Security' on it, as this is the hire company.   TINA is sitting just on the edge of her plot, on which a tub with a lid has appeared in the top corner.   They have been talking and now TINA is reading a book, that URSULA has lent her, called "The Marks and Spencer's Manifesto to growing your own food".

URSULA: There.   Try and sabotage my plot now.

TINA: I still think you should say something to them.

URSULA: It's a waste of time.   They all stick up for each other, even Richard.   But they haven't beaten me yet.

She takes a piece of camouflage and drapes it over the camera.

TINA: This book makes it sound quite easy.

URSULA: It is, as long as you don't have anyone interfering.

TINA: Where did you get it?

URSULA: Mark's.   You can borrow it if you like.

TINA: I'd like to grow my own food.

URSULA: Why don't you then?   Plant some seeds, assume control.   By the time they realise what you're doing it will be too late to stop you.

TINA: True.   I think I will borrow this.

URSULA: What's in the tub?

TINA: Don't know.

URSULA: What do you mean you don't know?

TINA: I didn't put it there.

URSULA: Then who did?

TINA: I don't know.

URSULA: Well take a look.

TINA: *(Unconcerned)* OK

> *TINA goes over to the tub and peers inside.*

TINA: Hmm.

URSULA: Well?

TINA: Caterpillars.

URSULA: Caterpillars?   Well we don't want them in here, they'll
                 eat everything.

TINA: We can't just get rid of them, they must belong to
someone.

URSULA: Too bad, kill them.

TINA: I'm not killing them.   They'd make an awful mess for a
                 start.

URSULA: They'll make a mess anyway, might as well do it now.

TINA: No, no, wait.   Let's at least see what they're doing in
                 here, eh?

URSULA: I bet Amy's behind this.

TINA: Funny looking little things, not like any caterpillars I've ever seen.

URSULA: Just put the lid on, if your not going to squash them OK.

TINA looks at URSULA in disgust and replaces the lid.
AMY enters, she is obviously distressed. She goes straight to her plot and pours herself a drink. She sits, wide eyed, staring at the floor.

TINA: Are you alright?

AMY pours herself another drink.

URSULA: What's the idea of putting these caterpillars near my plot?

TINA narrows her eyes at URSULA, in disbelief at he lack of compassion.
URSULA tut's and dismissively gets on with tending her plot.
RICHARD enters. He too has a sense of urgency about him.

RICHARD: *(Concerned, to Amy)* I came down as soon as I heard. He was a friend of yours wasn't he?

AMY nods.

RICHARD: Is there anything I can do? I feel so bad, I mean he was one of our best customers.

URSULA: *(Suddenly curious)* What's happened?

RICHARD: Oh what do you care?

AMY pours herself another drink.

AMY: *(Vaguely)* I only spoke with him the other day. It's all my fault.

RICHARD goes over and puts his arm around her.

RICHARD: Amy, these things happen sometimes, we can't blame ourselves.

TINA: What is it?

RICHARD: I just feel so bad that it happened on his way up to the bank.

URSULA: Has something happened to Brian?

AMY: *(Bitterly)* Oh you'd like that wouldn't you?

RICHARD: One of Amy's close friends has been in an accident.

TINA: What sort of accident?

RICHARD: He fell down a lift shaft, does it matter?

URSULA: Which floor?

The others all looks at URSULA. AMY bursts out crying.

TINA: You poor thing.

RICHARD: Would you like me to take you home Amy?

She shakes her head.

URSULA: *(Walking straight onto Amy's plot)* I'm sorry to hear about your friend, OK, but I'm not having caterpillars in here. For a start we're not supposed to have any pets...

AMY: Did I invite you onto my plot? *(She picks up the gnome).* Did we invite her Leon?

URSULA: If I tell them you've got pets, you're for it.

RICHARD: I really don't think this is the time Ursula!

URSULA: You don't scare me, 'Dick'.

AMY pours another drink cuddling Leon.
JAN enters, she is in a good mood, whistling. Under her arm she has a Mulberry bush. She walks straight onto TINA's plot and places it down beside the tub. Seeing this TINA and URSULA look at each other quizzically.

TINA: Are those your caterpillars?

JAN: Not just any old caterpillars: Silk Worms. Getting a bit cold for them outside, and this'll save me a fortune *(referring to the bush).*

TINA: What are they doing on my plot?

JAN: *(Looking into the tub)* Just wriggling about.

TINA: I mean: What are they doing, there?

JAN: *(Astonished she is being questioned)* You don't expect me to keep them outside do you?

URSULA: Yes.

JAN: I'm not asking you.

TINA: You certainly didn't ask me.

JAN: We didn't think you'd mind.

URSULA: Well she does.

TINA: *(A little awkwardly)* I'd rather you didn't keep them
               there, OK?

JAN: They hardly take up any room, you haven't exactly done
               anything here have you? What's more I'm letting you
               have this *(referring to the bush)*. It's a mulberry bush.
               Obviously I'll help you look after it.

        BRIAN enters, he walks straight over to AMY purposefully.

BRIAN: Amy, I'm so sorry to hear about Mr. Wolf.

URSULA: *(To Brian)* Did you tell Jan she could...

AMY: *(Vaguely, to Brian)* Apparently they were doing some
               maintenance work, they were on their tea break.

        *BRIAN totally ignores URSULA and rushes over to comfort AMY.
        Seeing his approach RICHARD stands aside.*

JAN: *(Noticing for the first time).* What's happened?

TINA: One of Amy's friends just died.

JAN: How?

URSULA: Down the elevator shaft - splat!

        AMY wails again.

RICHARD: Are you completely heartless, or just completely stupid?

AMY: *(Through the tears)* Oh just ignore her.

RICHARD: No, I won't just ignore her. Now I've only been a custodian here for a while, but already Ursula you are beginning to annoy me. I can quite see why the others wanted to get rid of you, because quite honestly you're a pain in the arse.

AMY, BRIAN and JAN's gazes flit about the Glasshouse, guiltily. URSULA stands solid, unmoved.

RICHARD: No-one wants to hear about your ridiculous ideas...

URSULA: I wouldn't be too sure of that.

The other custodians look around at each other, until all eyes fall on TINA.

TINA: *(Timidly)* Erm, actually I quite like some of her ideas.

AMY: What!

BRIAN: Oh, this is ridiculous, we're reducing ourselves to some common archaic allotment.

JAN: *(Referring to Tina)* I told you she had no idea...

AMY: *(To Tina)* How could you?

URSULA: Perhaps you should try it Richard?

RICHARD: Never, never! *(He turns to the others)* Is this what we want? Well, is it? The whole Glasshouse turned into a cabbage patch? And we are to be Cabbage-Garden Patriots? *(Cowards).*

BRIAN: What's the point, when we can grow everything we need artificially? I don't understand why...

TINA: And I don't understand why you can't just let her get on with it. It's nothing to do with the rest of you.

RICHARD: But that's where you're wrong, she wants to turn every single plot in here the same way. She even tried to get me to join in this madness. If you don't believe me ask her, go on.

Pause.

BRIAN: Well?

URSULA: I don't make a secret of the fact I think this whole 'modus operandi', is nothing more than an outdated, elitist league of has-beens.

AMY: How dare you!

BRIAN: Well, I think that's clear enough. And, perhaps if you cannot speak civily to us, it's better we do not speak at all.

URSULA closes her mouth smugly and turns back, to work on cultivating her plot.
BRIAN grits his teeth.

RICHARD: Well said Brian.

BRIAN: I don't need your compliments, thankyou very much!

RICHARD: Sorry, I was just...

BRIAN: And what are you doing on this plot anyway?

RICHARD: I thought Amy needed some...

BRIAN: That's your plot, over there. Kindly remember your place here.

RICHARD: I was only...

BRIAN: You can't wander around willy nilly, my God man where
              would we be if everyone did that?

TINA: I have a point of order actually.

RICHARD: I simply wanted to...

BRIAN: Kindly leave this plot.

TINA: Are we allowed to put things on other people's land?

RICHARD: I'm sorry to bring this up Brian, but this isn't your
              domain.

TINA: I mean like containers, bushes, that sort of thing?

BRIAN: *(Still to Richard, still agitated)* What do you mean?

JAN: *(To Tina)* They're not interested.

RICHARD: I mean: This is Amy's plot, doesn't she have a say?

JAN: We're too far away for them to worry.

RICHARD: Surely it is up to her who stays?

TINA: *(Calling to the others)* Hello.

BRIAN: *(To Amy)* Will you tell this idiot to get back on his own
              turf?

RICHARD: I didn't see you receive an invite.

AMY: For goodness sake, both of you get off!

RICHARD/BRIAN: What?

AMY: I'm fed up with people taking advantage of me. From now on plot 001 is out of bounds.

BRIAN: Out of bounds?

JAN: But not to me?

AMY: Doesn't anybody care about my space? About my feelings? "Oh, let's all go over to Amy's, the grass is always greener over there". I know you're all jealous of the fact that I've got the best plot, but it hasn't always been like this you know. I've had to work. Have you any idea how hard it has been to get the lawn to look like this?

TINA: Didn't we design some sort of water sprinkler system for you?

AMY: And I suppose you think that gives you the right to come over here and trample it all down do you?

TINA: Well, no but...

AMY: Just because your company happen to have helped me out, doesn't give you the right to set up camp here.

TINA: I've never even been on your plot.

AMY: The demands that are made on me.

BRIAN: But you said you loved visitors?

AMY: Can't you understand, I need space of my own?

BRIAN: Of course we do but...

AMY: Then respect my privacy.

The two men stand for a moment, then shuffle off dejectedly.
BRIAN returns to his plot for a moment, he picks up a trowel and
looks around for something to do.   Frustrated he throws it to the
ground and walks out.   RICHARD calls after him, concerned.

RICHARD: Brian, Brian!

RICHARD goes after BRIAN to calm him down.
URSULA shakes her head in amusement and exits with a watering
can.
JAN walks closer to AMY's plot.

JAN: Amy?   You didn't mean... not me as well?   Did you?

Silence, as AMY swigs another drink.   JAN grits her teeth in
resentment.

JAN: *(Innocently, to Tina, but loud enough for Amy to hear)*
                        Funny really, in all the years I've been in this building,
                        I've never known anyone to fall down a lift shaft.

TINA: *(A little surprised she is being included in a conversation)*
                        Oh, really?

JAN: Yes.   I didn't see a circular, there's always a circular, if
                        they're doing maintenance work.

AMY's ears prick up.

JAN: It's all a bit strange, don't you think?

TINA: Now you come to mention it...

JAN: Almost as if someone had it in for poor old Mr. Wolf, eh?
                        I mean, people don't step into empty lift shafts, do they?

AMY: What are you getting at?

JAN: Getting at, me?

AMY: What are you trying to say?

JAN: Just commenting on a bizarre accident, that's all.   I mean, it's not as if anyone would have wanted him dead, is it?

TINA: I didn't even know the man.

JAN: Me neither.   But if I had been a friend of his, say a close friend, I'd be worried.

TINA: Worried, what ever for?

JAN: In case I knew, or I'd put him up to it.

TINA: Up to what?

JAN: Well I don't know - I'm speaking hypothetically of course.

TINA: Of course.

JAN: But if someone had pushed poor old Mr. Wolf, what would stop them coming after me?

TINA: First blood and all that?

JAN: Precisely.   Once he'd tasted blood...

AMY: Stop it!

TINA: Oh Amy, I'm sorry, he was your friend wasn't he?

JAN: *(Smirking)* I'd completely forgotten.

AMY looks towards the door uneasily.

TINA: *(Whispering to JAN)* Perhaps we'd better not talk about
                it, eh?

JAN smiles.

TINA: Now, we're going to have to sort out these silk worms...

JAN: *(Grabbing Tina by the throat, whispering)* If you touch
                one of my caterpillars, or that bloody mulberry bush, I'll
                break every bone in your body - understand?

*She releases TINA and pushes past her out of the door. TINA
stands motionless.*

INTERVAL

Scene Six: The Glasshouse: A few days later.

It is pouring with rain outside.   JAN stands beside the mulberry bush, weeding.
BRIAN enters, carrying a bottle of wine, he walks towards his own plot.   As he passes Tina's plot he catches JAN out of the corner of his eye.   Curiously he stops and turns to face her.

BRIAN:	What are you doing?
JAN:	A spot of weeding, thought I'd get down here early.
BRIAN:	Does Tina know you're on here?
JAN:	Of course.
BRIAN:	And she's happy for you to be 'weeding'.
JAN:	It's my bush.
BRIAN:	Yours? Then what's it doing on Tina's plot?
JAN:	Don't be silly Brian, I haven't got room for mulberry bushes on my plot: I've barely got enough room to stand on it. And look at the weather.
BRIAN:	How long's it been there.
JAN:	About a week.

BRIAN thinks for a moment, he looks outside.

BRIAN:	You do realise this makes things very difficult.
JAN:	In what way?

- 47 -

BRIAN: Well, if you and Tina have come to some arrangement...
                where does that leave the rest of us?

JAN: Exactly where you are Brian.

*As BRIAN puzzles over this answer AMY swans in.   She is wearing
a personal stereo, the music loud enough for the others to hear.
She also has an assortment of games and books (solitaire etc., all
designed for one person).
Forgetting JAN for a moment, BRIAN follows AMY to the boarder
of her plot, like a lap dog.   He hesitates as AMY strolls onto her
plot.   She stops, noticing him hovering for the first time.
BRIAN lifts up the bottle of wine and holds it towards AMY,
tapping the side and smiling.*

AMY: *(Removing her headphones momentarily)*   No thanks,
                I've given up.

*BRIAN snarls and traipses over to his plot.   AMY looks over at
JAN, who is still working happily.*

AMY: *(Casually)*   Oh, by the way, you seem to be flooded.

JAN: What!

*She runs out of the Glasshouse to see her plot.   AMY replaces her
headphones.
After a moment AMY looks over at BRIAN, who is weeding his own
plot and repairing some of the damage.   She turns down her
headphones, so she can hear him.*

AMY: Brian?

BRIAN: *(Pleased that she is speaking to him)*   Yes?

AMY: I wanted a word with you.

BRIAN: Certainly, what is it?

AMY: It's about... well I'm not happy with the way things are...

BRIAN: Me neither. We're old friends, not just colleagues. I
                like to think we have a sort of 'special relationship',
                closer than the others.

AMY: Quite. And we can rise above any bitterness or
                resentment over what has happened.

BRIAN: Absolutely.

        Pause.

AMY: Has the insurance company paid out yet?

BRIAN: No, they've contested the claim, as expected.

AMY: Pity.

BRIAN: Yes.

AMY: I've always admired the way you handle things, situations,
                you know. Fran's a lucky woman.

BRIAN: Thank you. It's our silver wedding anniversary next
                week.

AMY: Oh, congratulations. *(Returning to the point at hand)* I
                was thinking particularly of when Bill went on the
                rampage...

BRIAN: Oh, that.

AMY: The way you stopped him dead in his tracks, laid down
                the law, really gave him something to think about.

BRIAN: *(Modestly)* Well..

AMY: Certainly made an impression on him: Snapped that shovel clean in two.

BRIAN: *(Defensively)* If he hadn't been running there would have been a lot less re-constructive surgery.   At the point of impact his face was definitely over the boarder.

AMY: Of course I know that, I was here, but do you think Richard does?

BRIAN: How do you mean?

AMY: Do you think he might feel that you used excessive force?

BRIAN: The man was on the rampage.

AMY: Sixteen hours on the operating table, apparently.

BRIAN: If this is about Jan's wild accusation, regarding the lift shaft incident, it won't wash with me.   For a start I don't think Richard has it in him and, even if he did, do you think I would be frightened of him?

AMY: Obviously not.

BRIAN: Besides, from what I've heard, he's on a bit of a sticky wicket at the moment anyway: Over stretched his means.   That's partially why the insurance company's holding out.   You can't tell me a man who's in personal financial trouble can remain manager of a bank for too long.

A wry smile lights his face.   AMY thinks for a moment.

AMY: About that shovel.

BRIAN: Yes?

AMY: Have you replaced it?

BRIAN: Not yet, you know how expensive tools are?

AMY: But it was my shovel, wasn't it?

BRIAN: Was it?

AMY: Yes, don't you remember? You said, 'Give us that shovel you dozy bitch'.

BRIAN: Did I?

AMY: Then you smacked him one.

BRIAN: Well yes, but it was in the heat of battle I...

AMY: Doesn't help me when I need to dig something up though does it Brian.

BRIAN: You never used it, it was brand new.

AMY: All the more reason I'd like a replacement. No rush, couple of days, whatever. I hear there's an auction next Tuesday, you might pick one up there.

She turns her headphones back up and starts to read. BRIAN is livid, but cannot decide what to do. He paces up and down the boarder like a trapped Lion, it's food on the other side.
JAN enters, soaking wet, holding a fishing net full of grass.

JAN: It's a bloody disaster, half my top soil's been washed clean away. It's going to cost me a fortune to sort this out.

*TINA enters. Giving JAN a wide birth she goes onto her plot.
She looks at the soil in disbelief.*

TINA: Who's pulled up all my vegetables?

She looks at JAN, who raises the net menacingly.

BRIAN: You said they were weeds?

JAN: Oh how was I to know the difference.

TINA: You've ruined my whole crop, two packets of seeds that
                    was.

BRIAN: How dare you pull up plants on someone else's land!

JAN: *(Ignoring Brian)* Amy, Amy!

AMY lifts one earpiece to listen.

JAN: I don't suppose you could give me an advance on those
                    dresses, I need to get some more top soil.

AMY: I'm sorry Jan *(Replacing the earpiece).*

BRIAN: Are you listening to me?

*TINA moves towards the mulberry bush but JAN stamps her foot
and TINA retreats.*

TINA: *(To Brian)* And she's left this tub of caterpillars here.

BRIAN: This is outrageous.

JAN: Oh shut up Brian.

BRIAN is lost for words.

JAN: What are you going to do, hit me in the face with a shovel? Now, the caterpillars and the bush stay. That's all I'm asking. And, as long as they come to no harm, that's all I want. *(She throws the net of damp grass onto Tina's plot).* As it's obvious no-one's offering to help me, if you'll excuse me, I have some work to do re-building my plot.

JAN exits.

TINA: You can't just let her...

BRIAN: *(Deflated)* What can I do?

BRIAN returns to his own plot. TINA looks at the bush angrily.

TINA: Right then, I'll just have to move north.

She starts to rip out the grass and weeds in the northern corner of her plot. Seeing this AMY pulls her headphones off.

AMY: What are you doing?

TINA: Making more room for my vegetables.

AMY: But it'll look so ugly. There'll be a vast expanse of mud, spreading over the eastern side of the Glasshouse.

URSULA enters, she is carrying two boxes of chemical fertiliser. AMY hastily replaces her headphones.

URSULA: And we don't want too much mud do we? Or people will realise we can all grow things ourselves.

TINA: Jan's pulled up all my vegetables. I don't suppose I could borrow a couple of packets of seeds?

URSULA:	I'm sorry, but I'm having to re-think things, I won't have anything spare. Of course you could always ask Amy for some seeds, but then I'm not sure her vegetables have them.
TINA:	She doesn't grow food.
URSULA:	Not up here, but her company's just developed a new cloning method for artificially produced vegetables and fruit.

BRIAN has overheard this and is curious.

URSULA:	Double the yield in half the time.
BRIAN:	Amy's?
URSULA:	Yes. I thought you, of all people, would have heard. She's just won a contact to supply the Ocean Group.
BRIAN:	The... but they were one of my best customers.

BRIAN storms over to AMY's plot a rips off her headphones.

BRIAN:	What the hell are you doing producing vegetables?
AMY:	I... well... One has to diversify to survive Brian.
BRIAN:	What about me? What about my survival?
AMY:	Business is business.
BRIAN:	Bullshit. We bought all our equipment from you, you know I can't afford to upgrade it at the moment.
AMY:	Precisely. Unfortunately that's the nature of technology Brian, things change, suddenly you're left behind. I knew you couldn't afford to replace all your equipment,

that's why I didn't bother you. It just so happened it was easier to set up a subsidiary, for the green groceries. We'll probably float it on the stock market soon, I'll let you in on some shares.

BRIAN: How could you? How could you do this to me?

AMY: It's a hard world Brian.

BRIAN: Then why make it any harder?

BRIAN returns to his plot, crest fallen, and continues tidying up. AMY, feeling a little guilty, puts her headphones back on. URSULA has been taking up all her plants, watched by TINA.

TINA: Why are you pulling everything up?

URSULA: It's not growing fast enough. If things are going to work they must fit into an overall plan, you can't leave it to nature - at least not at first.

TINA: But I thought we were trying to grow organic food.

URSULA: Eventually, yes. But it just doesn't seem practical at the moment. With this new method of cultivation Amy's factories can produce one fully ripe courgette in ten seconds. Ten seconds, have you any idea what that means?

TINA: Yes, courgettes every night for dinner, or a pile of rotting veg.

URSULA: Look, I would never, ever go to producing soilless plants. It's totally against my ethics, we have to get out of this cycle of 'artificial cultivation'. But we can only do that by forcing our plants on. It's what these things were designed for *(referring to the Glasshouse).*

TINA: *(Looking at the fertiliser)* And you are prepared to use any means?

URSULA: It's only a bit of fertiliser, simply to start things off. I'm giving it five days and then I'll re-asses the situation.

TINA: What do you think I should do about Jan?

URSULA: I'm sorry Tina, but I'm far too busy. You'll have to fight your own battles.

URSULA returns to clearing her plot. TINA stands for a moment. Taking a packet of seeds from her pocket URSULA tosses them at Tina's feet.

URSULA: Here.

Scene Seven: The Glasshouse: The next morning.

RICHARD sits on his plot, he is fixing an old lawn mower.
BRIAN enters, his head is down and he is depressed.   He goes and
sits on his plot, head in hands.

RICHARD: Are you all right Brian?

BRIAN looks up and sees the lawnmower for the first time.   He is
a little surprised.

BRIAN: What are you doing with that?

RICHARD: It's a lawn mower.

BRIAN: I know what it is.   What are you doing with it?   You
              know you're forbidden to use any equipment.

RICHARD: Oh. I don't have any intention of using it.   It's a sort of
              hobby.

BRIAN: *(Suspiciously)* I see.

    Pause.

RICHARD: I'm sorry about the payout, things are a little tight at the
              moment.   Once I get on my feet again I'll be able to
              increase the payments, I'm sure.

BRIAN: Make sure you do.

RICHARD: Believe me, it's my first priority.   I feel terrible about the
              whole thing, I really do.

    BRIAN tends his plot.

RICHARD: *(Referring to his plot)*   What are you planning to do?

BRIAN: Me?   I was thinking of a small rose garden here, a few perennials - Hemerocallis, Iberis Sempervirens, Liriope Muscari - that sort of thing.   A Juniperus Horizontalis up there, then, down here, I want things like Ipheion Uniflorum.

RICHARD: What about lawn?

BRIAN: Absolutely, garden's not a garden without lawn, eh?   It's going to be hard to get it flat enough for bowls again though.

RICHARD: I love bowls.

BRIAN: This isn't the same as indoor you know, far more skill.

RICHARD: You need a bit more space though, for a proper green.   If we got together...

BRIAN: *(Suddenly distant again)*   We can't start joining plots you know.

RICHARD: I'm not saying join, simply share the same objectives. We could use both areas together when we wanted to, but still have our individual space.   Imagine if, for some reason, Ursula was replaced too, think of the green we'd have then.

BRIAN: You're forgetting we have a zone between us, that neither of us can use for his benefit.

RICHARD: But what about the mutual benefit of the house?   Surely that would be OK.

BRIAN: You mean a sort of co-operative, mutual use but individual ownership?

RICHARD: Sort of. Specified areas we could get together over, make use of the whole house, yet still have individual plots. The barriers could come down, we could be a real community.

TINA enters, she looks around for JAN then sneaks onto her plot. Around the Mulberry bush and caterpillar tub there are now a circle of stones. TINA pick up four stones and surreptitiously puts them into her pockets. She re-arranges the stones, so the circle is smaller. She sneaks out. BRIAN and RICHARD have watched with interest.

BRIAN: *(Realising he has been talking civily to Richard)* Completely out of the question of course.

RICHARD: What?

BRIAN: Firstly, due to a loss of customers, there's no way I can afford to do anything substantial to my plot at the moment. And secondly, do you really think a manageable agreement could be reached between us? Look at us, we're not a community and never will be.

AMY enters, she has another armful of new garden accessories, including a gnome sized deck chair. She walks over to her plot and sits down, placing Leon on the chair.

AMY: *(To Leon)* Glorious day today, don't you think Leon? Soda? *(She pours two drinks)* It's so nice to be able to relax in one's own space, unwind after the rigours of a busy day. If you'd have said to me yesterday that aubergines would have overtaken parsnips in popularity I wouldn't have believed it, yet today's figures are unequivocal, not that parsnips are doing badly.

BRIAN: Glad to see someone's doing alright.

AMY: Oh, hello Brian, Richard. Didn't see you there.

BRIAN turns away from her, but RICHARD remains a while.
Awkwardly he approaches the edge of her plot.

RICHARD: So, er... Things are going well then?

AMY: Swimmingly.

RICHARD: Grass needs a cut.

AMY: Heavens no. All that clattering and sweating, it finds it's own level eventually. Besides it gives some of the other plants a chance to grow, I've had all sorts springing up: Clover, dandelions, even mushrooms. I don't know where they come from. I haven't had to do any work on it.

BRIAN: Grass does not find its own level.

AMY: It gets to a point where it doesn't need cutting...

BRIAN: *(Under his breath)* Unlike your throat.

RICHARD: So you're not going to be growing any vegetables on your plot then?

AMY: Don't be absurd, far too much work, and what's the point?

RICHARD: My sentiments exactly.

AMY puts a pair of sunglasses on LEON.

RICHARD: Mind you, you're lucky here, you don't have to worry about them spreading - taking over your plot.

AMY: No.

RICHARD: Whereas I..., I have to watch my boundaries like a hawk.
                What with Ursula and now Tina falling victim to this
                'self sufficiency' craze.   I'm beginning to wonder if the
                idea itself is infectious, let alone the plants.

AMY: Yes, glad they're not next to me.

RICHARD: But then you said yourself, things sprout up all over the
                place.   Can't be too careful.

*AMY smiles in gratitude at RICHARD's caution then, bored with
him, turns her attentions back to LEON.   RICHARD walks about
her boarder, he bends down and picks something up.*

RICHARD: What's this?

AMY looks up.

RICHARD: Some sort of... caterpillar.

*AMY stands to take a closer look, she shrieks and slaps it from
RICHARD's hand, stamping on it.*

BRIAN: What is it?

RICHARD: A caterpillar.

BRIAN: Don't be ridiculous.

AMY: Where did it come from?

RICHARD: I don't know I just found it here.

AMY anxiously surveys the grass on her plot.

RICHARD: You see, how things appear.   Probably after the
            vegetables.

AMY: But I don't want vegetables, I like flowers and grass.

BRIAN: Vegetables have flowers, how do you think they get
            pollinated?

AMY: They start off harmlessly enough, but then they mutate
            into something quite different.

BRIAN: Oh, please.   There's nothing wrong with a bit of variety,
            it's healthy for the soil.

RICHARD: But things take over Brian, some plants are stronger than
            others.

BRIAN: So you cut them back.

AMY: But that would mean 'gardening', wouldn't it?   Can't you
            buy some sort of selective killer instead?

RICHARD: It wouldn't surprise me if these natural varieties gave off
            some kind of vapour that altered your state of mind, made
            you more likely to want to plough up the soil and grow
            your own food.   Probably be chicken coops next, and
            when they're ready to eat...*(He draws his hand across his
            throat)*.   And you know what they're like once they've
            had the chop, no controlling them, blood everywhere.

            *AMY looks disgusted as the thought of chicken's blood
            surrounding her haven of relaxation.*

RICHARD: As the amount of vegetables in here increase, the chances
            of you finding them sprouting on your plot grows by the
            same proportions.

AMY: Then you must do something to stop them spreading, you
                  must take adequate precautions.

RICHARD: Naturally I'd love to but, at the moment, I couldn't afford
                  to buy plant killer - it's only available on the black
                  market.

BRIAN: They'll be no plant killer in this Glasshouse, thankyou
                  very much.   Things are far too delicate as it is.

RICHARD: *(Confidentially to Amy)*   I know where to get hold of
                  some, but it's pricey.   Still, I reckon if I could stop them
                  spreading to my plot, you'd be alright.

AMY: Then you must get some.

RICHARD: Like I said, I'm in no position to think of getting it at the
                  moment, unless...

AMY: Yes.

RICHARD: Unless I could borrow some of that money I gave you.   I
                  could use it to get the stuff, and then pay you back when
                  I'm straight.

AMY: Alright, how much do you need?

BRIAN: *(Overhearing this last question)*   What's going on?

AMY: Nothing.

BRIAN: I thought you were refusing to get involved with the rest
                  of the house?

AMY: I...

BRIAN: And now you're going to lend him money?

AMY: Only until he can sort out his plot...

BRIAN: Money from my customers, may I add.

          Unseen TINA sneaks on, as before, and removes some more stones as...

AMY: It's my money Brian.

BRIAN: Well I'm sorry but I absolutely forbid it.

RICHARD: Who do you think you are?   You can't go ordering people around all the time Brian.

AMY: Richard please.

BRIAN: I don't need you to tell me what I can and can't do!   If I forbid it, then I forbid it.

RICHARD: But no-one needs to take any notice of you Brian.   Have you thought about that?   Has that thought ever crossed your arrogant imperialistic mind?

BRIAN: Me?   Imperialistic?   Ha!   It's you who suggested a conglomeration of estates.

RICHARD: Well perhaps I was mistaken, you obviously lack the personal inter-relationship skills to cohabit with your fellow humans courteously!

BRIAN: Oh bollocks.

          At the other side of the Glasshouse TINA is about to leave with pockets full of stones when JAN enters, carrying a dress box, as...

AMY: I think we've been here before haven't we?

RICHARD: Only because he still thinks he's got some hold over you.

BRIAN: I do not.

RICHARD: Oh come off it Brian, you treat her as if she owes you
             something, I know all about the affair.

BRIAN: I...

AMY: Look, it's up to me what I do with my money OK?   I
             don't need either of you to make any decisions for me.

*JAN shuffles left and right, blocking TINA's exit, until finally TINA
outwits her and makes a break for it.   JAN looks over at TINA's
plot suspiciously as...*

RICHARD: Good.   Then what are you going to do?

*AMY looks at RICHARD and BRIAN.
JAN checks the caterpillars.*

AMY: I'm sorry Richard.

*JAN checks the stones, she counts them as...
RICHARD exhales angrily.*

RICHARD: Fine.

*RICHARD returns to his plot.   URSULA enters.   BRIAN looks at
AMY with begrudged gratitude.*

URSULA: *(Looking at her plants)*   At last things are coming
             together.   Just a bit of careful planning and a little push in
             the right direction, that's all you need.

AMY: *(Shouting across to Ursula)* I'm not having your
                           headless chickens in here, there's rules about that sort of
                           thing you know!

URSULA: ?

*Realising her stones have been moved JAN exits abruptly, leaving
the dress box on her plot.*

AMY: Don't worry little Leon, we'll get rid of her.   Then you
                           can go back home, and maybe we'll get some little friends
                           for you to play with.

URSULA: Over my dead body.

AMY: That's what I was counting on.

*URSULA is about to launch herself at AMY but decides she cannot
be bothered.*

TINA: *(Off)* Ouch!

AMY: *(Still taunting Ursula)* I know you want to take over, I
                           know you've been spying on me with that camera.

URSULA: Why would I want to spy on you?   You're so transparent
                           we could cut a square out of you and stick it in the roof.

A mobile telephone starts to ring as...

AMY: I have friends in your company you know.

URSULA: You don't have any friends, just hangers on.

AMY: I do so have friends, and what's more I'm going to tell
                           them that you are ruining the whole atmosphere up here.
                           Things were peaceful before you came along.

URSULA: Get out of here.

BRIAN: Is that a phone I can hear?

*JAN returns carrying the stones TINA had taken from around the
bush. She starts to re-position them as...*

AMY: Agreed, we may have had our little differences but on the
              whole we all wanted the same thing.

URSULA: Elitism.

AMY: Don't we deserve a little relaxation, away from the rigours
              of work? Why is everything such a struggle with you?
              Can't you just sit and relax, let things be?

BRIAN: Amy.

AMY: Why do you have to bring the grey and dismal world
              below up here with you? Isn't that what we are trying to
              get away from?

BRIAN: Amy.

AMY: If you want to work, fine, but don't do it up here. This is
              supposed to be the domain of a privileged few. It might
              not be fair, but that's the way it is. People don't expect
              us to get our hands dirty, they're not asking us be like
              them. We're above all that, life goes on downstairs
              regardless of what we do. Why not just enjoy it while
              you can, instead of subjecting all of us to your chaotic and
              offensive lifestyle.

BRIAN: Amy! Your phone.

AMY: What? Oh, I'm sorry, I must've forgotten to turn it off.

She rummages in her bag for the phone.

BRIAN: No phones, no phones.   What'll it be next, televisions?

URSULA: Of course it's all right for her to ignore the rules.

BRIAN: Not at all.

AMY: Hello.   Yes.

BRIAN: I'll just wait until she's finished this call and then I'll...

JAN picks up the dress box and makes her way to AMY's plot as...

AMY: *(Alarmed)* My what?   How..., but how...

BRIAN: Ah, looks like bad news.

URSULA turns away in disgust at BRIAN's lack of conviction.
She mixes up some more fertiliser as...

AMY: Are they sure it's...   I don't see how they can say that...
          Fine.   Yeah, well you do that OK, make sure it's done.

She shuts off the phone and stands in stunned silence as JAN tries
to catch her eye by waving the dress box.

AMY: It seems some people have erm..., well they've.   Certain
          allergies have developed to my new process of vegetable
          production.

BRIAN: Is it serious?

AMY: I think they're going to close us down.

Scene Eight: The Glasshouse: The Next Day.

AMY, BRIAN and JAN sit at the table, a few bottles of wine stand in front of them, some empty, some full.   AMY swigs from one of the bottles.   There is an air of discomfort, particularly between AMY and JAN.

BRIAN: What's nice is, that through all this adversity, we can still sit down like civilised people and enjoy each others company.

Silence.

BRIAN: I'm glad we established this little club, helps keep things together.

Silence.

JAN: *(To Amy, without looking at her)*   Those dresses are one offs you know.   It's not as if I could sell them on else where.

AMY: *(Still slightly stunned)*   I think I can hold onto the core of the company, they can't touch that.

BRIAN: *(Trying to lighten the atmosphere)*   It's my silver wedding anniversary tomorrow, twenty-five years, imagine that.

Silence.   They all take a drink.
TINA enters, she limps to her plot.

JAN: *(Standing)*   Excuse me a moment would you.

TINA cowers away to the north end of her plot as JAN approaches. JAN stands guard over her mulberry bush and tub of caterpillars.

AMY: *(Whispering to Brian)* Look at her, anyone would think it was her plot.

BRIAN: What can we do? I've told her my position on it and she just ignored me.

AMY: And there's still no news from the owner.

BRIAN: Then there's nothing we can do.

AMY: But what about the rules?

BRIAN: Worthless coins, when the currency's been changed.

AMY: The thing is, if we let her get away with it, who knows where it might lead.

BRIAN: I've drawn up some papers for Richard and Ursula to sign, agreeing not to use the neutral zones for their own benefit in any way.

AMY: Good.

BRIAN: What about you? Are you going to be able to hold on to your plot?

AMY: It's not the first time I've had set backs, something'll turn up.

BRIAN: I hope so, if you went, there's certainly no hope for me.

URSULA rushes in urgently.

URSULA: Have you heard, the Chief Executive of Richard's bank's been hit by a bus!

BRIAN: No-one gets hit by busses any more.

URSULA: Try telling him that, he's out on the street oozing life, as we speak.

AMY, BRIAN and JAN rush out.

URSULA: *(To Tina)* Coming?

TINA: No, I don't think so.

URSULA: What's happened to your foot?

TINA: Jan dropped a stone on it.

URSULA shakes her head.

TINA: Can't you do something?

URSULA: I'm sorry Tina, but it's really not my problem. I have enough trouble keeping my own house in order, the committee keep wanting to know when other members can come up here.

TINA: But it's making things very difficult for me, I'm thinking of giving up on this whole self sufficiency idea.

URSULA: Oh well that's great isn't it, the first little problem and your giving up.

TINA: She nearly broke my foot.

URSULA: For goodness sake Tina, what do you expect me to do, beat her up for you?

TINA: Would you?

URSULA: Of course not, what do you take me for?

AMY, BRIAN and JAN return.

BRIAN: *(Continuing a previous conversation)* ...and his say
would be final.

JAN: Even though Richard's the Custodian?

BRIAN: Technically it doesn't make any difference, the land is
leased by the company not the individual. If there's to be
a new Chief Executive Officer, and he wants Richard out,
then that's it.

AMY: So we could be looking at a new Custodian?

BRIAN: Maybe the Chief Exec himself.

AMY: Hmm.

URSULA: Well, you all seem devastated with the tragic news.

BRIAN: Naturally it's a terrible loss...

AMY: But you can't look a gift horse in the mouth.

*JAN returns to TINA's plot, carefully checking the stones etc.
TINA retreats up to her corner again.*

AMY: What exactly is in that tub Jan?

JAN: Silk worms.

AMY: You mean, caterpillars?

JAN: Yes.

AMY: Oh this really is the last straw.

JAN looks puzzled. AMY walks dramatically back to her plot.
URSULA watched in amusement.

URSULA:　　For once I agree with you Amy, I think it's a bloody liberty.

A moments pause while BRIAN thinks of how to approach
URSULA.

BRIAN:　　Erm..., Ursula?

URSULA:　　Yes.

BRIAN:　　Would you mind coming down here a moment?

URSULA cautiously approaches BRIAN, who produces a piece of paper from his pocket.

URSULA:　　What's this?

BRIAN:　　It's just an agreement, that's all.

URSULA:　　You're not having any more of my land.

BRIAN:　　No, no. Quite the contrary. We've drawn up agreements to prevent anyone else's land being taken. Read it, by all means. It actually refers to the buffer zones, the Custodian of Richard's plot will be signing one as well.

URSULA:　　*(Referring to Jan)* What about her?

BRIAN:　　Erm, yes, yes... possibly.

URSULA:　　What do I get out of it?

BRIAN: You, well erm... It seems so ridiculous that we're all in this together and, well quite frankly we have a sort of wine club...

AMY: You're not asking her to join?

BRIAN: I think it's time we put our differences behind us. *(Then quietly to Amy)* We need all the friends we can get.

URSULA: A wine club you say?

BRIAN nods. URSULA looks back at the buffer zone.

URSULA: *(Optimistically)* Alright, why not?

BRIAN hands her a pen and she signs the piece of paper, from his pocket he produces a membership card.

BRIAN: Here, you're officially a member. Now, we meet every Sunday...

BRIAN is stopped dead by the sight of RICHARD wheeling in the wheel barrow, full of rocks.

RICHARD: *(Jolly)* I hope you don't mind me using the wheel barrow, these are bloody heavy.

He stops at his plot and starts to unload them.

AMY: I thought you didn't have any money?

RICHARD: Yes well I've just been promoted.

BRIAN: Promoted?

RICHARD: Chief Executive Officer, haven't you heard? Shame about old Paul, still every cloud has a silver lining eh?

Seizing her moment, while everyone else is distracted, TINA takes some stones from around the mulberry bush and dashes out with them as...

AMY: But yesterday you were only a manager...

RICHARD: I know, I didn't realise I was so popular.

URSULA: *(Suspiciously)* How lucky you are Richard.

RICHARD: Unbelievable isn't it?

He exits cheerily.

JAN: You're not telling me that's not suspicious?

BRIAN: Jan please, there's nothing to suggest.

URSULA: No-one moves up from manager to Chief Executive Officer.

BRIAN: All I'm saying is we don't know the facts...

JAN: The fact is we're cohabiting with a murderer.

AMY: *(Grabbing Leon)* Oh Leon, what are we to do?

BRIAN: Let's not get hysterical, what happens at the bank is nothing to do with us. We simply have to get on with things up here.

RICHARD re-enters, carrying a large box labelled 'Vegi-Kill'. URSULA looks at it in horror.

BRIAN: Erm, Richard?

RICHARD: Yes.

BRIAN: Officially of course you've always been a member, but I haven't given you one of these.

He hands RICHARD a membership card.

RICHARD: What's this, oh the wine club. Thankyou Brian.

The others raise their eyes in dismay.

BRIAN: We meet every Sunday.

RICHARD: Sundays, right.

BRIAN: There is one more thing.

RICHARD: Yes.

BRIAN: *(Producing an agreement from his pocket)* I wonder if you'd care to sign one of these.

RICHARD takes it and reads it through quickly.

RICHARD: Sure.

BRIAN: *(Handing him a pen)* It's to protect the neutral zones.

RICHARD: Great. Anything else?

BRIAN: Not at the moment.

RICHARD hands BRIAN's pen back and starts to unload and position the rocks onto his plot.
There is a moment of awkward silence between the others.

BRIAN: Right, well I'd better be getting along then.

AMY: *(Urgently)* I'll come with you.

They leave.
URSULA looks at RICHARD, he stares back at her. She taps the
surveillance camera and looks down at his box of Vegi-Kill.
Taking her watering can she exits.
JAN and RICHARD watch her go. RICHARD returns to sorting
his rocks.

JAN: Killer.

RICHARD: What?

JAN: Killer, in that box?

RICHARD: Oh this, I hate vegetables.

JAN: Me too.

RICHARD: You have to think about the aesthetics of gardening. You
                can't simply plant things here and there. Landscaping,
                different levels, that's what you need.

JAN: I've got this plan, for this plot. It's a sort of rock garden,
                with a few alpine plants. I'd run a line in from the pond,
                so you could have a cascading waterfall, or maybe a rock
                pool. Over here I'd have a few bonsai and a grapevine.
                This area would be good for a lawn...

RICHARD: Striped?

JAN: Yeah, why not. You can do things with a bit of space.

RICHARD: Tell me about it. If I had a bit more space, just a bit of
                Brian's plot say, I could really do something then. I
                mean look at Amy's plot, what a waste. She's got lawn
                sure, but look at the state of it.

JAN: Her 'Laisse-fair' attitude annoys me.

RICHARD: If you're going to have a lawn do it properly: All the
                grass the same height, stripes you can be proud of, no
                dandelions or clover. I hate dandelions, don't you?
                They always do so well, prosper, wherever they are.
                Before you know it they've flowered and their seeds are
                off with the wind. I'd like to take each seed and crush it
                under my heel, until the whole species is wiped out. I've
                got some Dandy-Kill downstairs. There are some plants
                we simply don't need.

JAN: Even Tina's growing veg now.

RICHARD: I had a quick look earlier, courgettes I think. Course they
                spread like wild fire, once they take off there's no
                stopping them. Somewhere like this you'd be over run
                before you knew it.

                *JAN turns in a fit of anger and stamps on all TINA's plants
                maniacally. RICHARD watches with interest. When she has
                finished she wipes her brow and calmly turns back to him.*

JAN: You have to be careful.

RICHARD: Absolutely. They know no boundaries, those tendrils
                would be snaking their way round here at night when no-
                one was watching...

JAN: That's the trouble with vegetables, you can't trust them.

RICHARD: And they're so ugly.

JAN: Exactly. They have their place, and that's on the shelves
                at the supermarket.

RICHARD: People don't seem to understand that.   This could be
            beautiful up here, a garden of Eden, if they'd let someone
            plan it who knows what they're doing.

JAN: You're talking about landscaping the whole house?

RICHARD: I'm saying we need to get rid of this ridiculous vegetable
            growing commune idea and plan a garden.

JAN: I'm all for that.

RICHARD holds out his hand.

RICHARD: An anti-Communist pact?

JAN shakes his hand enthusiastically.
*TINA appears at the doorway, she is surprised to see the two of
them shaking hands.   She sees the damage to her plot and scurries
away.*

<u>Scene Nine: The Glasshouse: Two days later.</u>

*The Glasshouse appears empty.   The camouflage has gone from
URSULA's camera and lies in a bundle at the top corner of
TINA's plot, the caterpillar tub is empty and upside down, the
stones higgldy piggldy.   URSULA's plot is unchanged.
RICHARD's plot has been extended over the buffer zone and now
nearly borders BRIAN's.   BRIAN's plot remains unchanged.
AMY's plot is also apparently unaltered but LEON lies on the
grass with an ice pick buried into his head.
RICHARD enters pushing the wheel barrow, full of more plants,
tools etc.   He starts to unpack them onto his plot.
URSULA enters, she is obviously in a good mood, full of
confidence.*

URSULA: Morning Richard.

RICHARD: *(Warily)*   Good morning.

URSULA: Beautiful day, don't you think?

RICHARD: Yes, yes I suppose it is.

AMY enters carrying a fish bowl and a stand.

URSULA: Morning.

AMY: *(Unnerved)*   What?

URSULA: Just saying good morning.

AMY: Oh, right.   Hi.

AMY sets up the bowl on the stand, on the far side of her plot.

AMY: *(Quietly, in confidence)* Say, if Brian comes in, do me a favour would you - don't mention his anniversary: He found out yesterday that Fran's been having an affair.

RICHARD and URSULA nod sagely. AMY picks up a watering can and exits again.
Unable to contain herself any longer Ursula bursts out laughing.

RICHARD: You're very jolly this morning.

URSULA: Yes, I feel like a weight's been lifted from my shoulders, at last I'm free to make the decisions I need to, no more endless discussions.

AMY re-enters with a full watering can and a polythene bag containing a gold fish as...

URSULA: As of yesterday I dissolved the committee, it was getting such a bore.

AMY: You can't just 'dissolve' a committee.

URSULA: Obviously they'll be re-instated again, once things are running smoothly.   But they were holding things up, you can't have that when your dealing with organic commodities.   We were lacking direction as a company, so I've stepped in as Managing Director.

AMY hurries back to her plot.   She fills the bowl and empties the fish carefully in as...

RICHARD: So what happened to your 'co-operative' ideals.

URSULA: Like I said, nothing's changed.   I'm simply running the company that's all.

A devilish smile lights RICHARD's face.

BRIAN enters sullenly, carrying a miniature potted rose.

RICHARD: Morning Brian, how was the anniversary?

BRIAN narrows his eyes at Richard.
JAN enters, she is slightly shaken.

JAN: I erm..., has anyone... I was feeding the fish just now and suddenly... something appeared from under the water, took a mouth full of food and disappeared again.

BRIAN: Are you sure?

JAN: I know what I saw Brian.

RICHARD: It's a cat-fish.

JAN: A what?

RICHARD: A cat-fish, I saw it yesterday in the pet shop, I couldn't resist it.

AMY: So you put it in the pond?

RICHARD: Its seemed the best place for it, I didn't think you'd mind Jan, sorry if it gave you a fright.

AMY: *(Expecting him to reprimand Richard)* Brian?

BRIAN: Erm..., you can't expect us to pay for food for your cat-fish.

RICHARD: I wouldn't dream of it, I've bought some food as well, I thought we could share it.

AMY: But he's not supposed to have any fish in there.

BRIAN: I suppose if it's a shared thing...

JAN: I don't mind, now I know what it is.

AMY: We don't care what you think, it's the principal.

BRIAN: I think we have to put things into perspective here...

AMY: *(Referring to her fish)* What if I wanted to put Pearl in there, when she's a little bigger?

JAN: You're not putting that in there, it'll be overcrowded.

AMY: I shall go through the proper channels.

JAN: You'll go through the side window if you try and put that fish in my pond.

BRIAN: It is not your pond, your plot simply happens to be in the middle of it.

BRIAN turns towards his own plot and sees RICHARD's extension.

BRIAN: What's this?

RICHARD: I need a bit more space so...

BRIAN: You signed a piece of paper!

RICHARD: That wasn't for this buffer zone was it?

BRIAN: Yes.

RICHARD: I thought it was the other one.

BRIAN: Both, both.

RICHARD: But this used to be my land didn't it, I didn't think you meant this one.   Anyway I've left a bit of it there.

AMY: Richard you can't go moving your borders like that.

JAN sees her caterpillar tub for the first time.

JAN: What's happened to my caterpillars!   Tina!!

BRIAN: *(Still talking to Richard)*   You'll have to move them back again.

JAN: Tina, I'll kill you.

RICHARD: Oh come on Brian, I've planted things there now.

JAN rushes out.

AMY: Now you're taking liberties.

BRIAN: Are you going to move them or not?

RICHARD: Well..., I can't dig them up now, if you'd said something earlier.

BRIAN: Fine.

BRIAN takes his rose onto his plot.

URSULA: You're not letting him get away with it, are you?

BRIAN: If the plants are established it seems a shame to uproot them.

URSULA: But...

BRIAN: However there will be no more concessions in this house.

AMY: What about the fish?

RICHARD: *(To Ursula)* It was my land to start with.

URSULA: What about my land?   I want mine back as well.

BRIAN: Out of the question, the matter is closed.

>   *JAN returns with a spade, held weapon like.   She looks around for*
>   *TINA then takes position on her plot.*

BRIAN: Jan, what are you doing?

JAN: I'm taking over plot 005, it's the only way to protect my
                  interests.

AMY: You can't simply march onto someone else's land.

JAN: I'd like to see her try and stop me.

BRIAN: Get off there at once!

RICHARD: *(Looking at the small buffer zone left between him and*
                  Brian) Its seems a shame to leave that bit barren.

>   *AMY discovers LEON.*

AMY: Arrg!

BRIAN: What is it?

AMY: Somebody's murdered Leon, look he's got an ice pick in
                  his head!

>   *RICHARD starts to move his boarder right to the edge of BRIAN's*
>   *plot.*

URSULA: Look, look he's moving his boarder!

BRIAN and AMY turn back.

RICHARD: It seems ridiculous not to have this bit as well.

AMY: *(Pointing accusingly at Ursula)* It was you, wasn't it?

URSULA: Oh it's only a stupid gnome.

AMY: Murderer.

BRIAN: Now Richard, you agreed. This isn't the behaviour of a gentleman, or a member of the wine club.

RICHARD: Actually Brian, I hate wine.

He hands him back the membership card.

AMY: This is anarchy!

JAN: Oh shut up Amy.

AMY: How dare you tell me to shut up.

BRIAN: Let's just all calm down and sort this out.

URSULA: I want some of my land back.

JAN: *(Putting down the shovel and tearing up her membership card)* I don't think I want to be a member of anything that includes 'her' either.

AMY: You know what? I never did like those dresses Jan, and I'm not surprised you can't get rid of them.

URSULA: I said, I want some of my land back Brian.

BRIAN: Everything I ever worked for has crashed into ruins.

RICHARD: What's it got to do with him, it's between our plots.

BRIAN: If you attempt to enter that buffer zone this means war!

JAN: *(To Amy)* It's a good job you're so far away, otherwise I'd...

TINA leaps out, from under the camouflage, screaming and knocks JAN to the floor.

BRIAN: Ursula I appeal to you as a fellow member of the wine club.

URSULA tosses her membership card onto the floor.

URSULA: I'm sorry Brian.

She shakes hands with RICHARD.

RICHARD: Fifty fifty?

URSULA nods and starts to move her things into her side of the buffer zone. RICHARD exits.

BRIAN: I'm warning you, we won't stand for this!

AMY: *(Distressed)* This day will be a day that will live in infamy.

JAN manages to throw TINA off, struggle to her feet and pick up a stone.

RICHARD charges in with the lawn mower as...

RICHARD: There's going to be a New Order in here Brian!

AMY:　　　　　Look out Tina!

TINA pushes JAN over as...

BRIAN:　　　　*(Launching himself at Richard)*　This is war!

URSULA:　　　　Get him Richard!

JAN staggers to her feet and raises the stone, AMY ducks.

AMY:　　　　　No Jan, not Pearl!!

JAN hurls the stone across the Glasshouse, knocking the fish bowl off its stand.

Blackout.

SOUNDTRACK: Glass breaking.

Ends.

Other Plays by the same author include:

THE THIEFTAKER

SMOKE

BOOM

EXTENSIONS OF LOVE

THE SNOW QUEEN

WORLDS APART

THE LITTLE MERMAID

www.darrenrapier.co.uk

DARREN RAPIER

Darren Rapier trained at Rose Bruford College, graduating in 1995 with a degree in writing. He has written for film, television and theatre. Plays include *The Thieftaker,* about the first real gangster in early Eighteenth Century London; *People in Glass Houses*, a futuristic absurd comedy; *Smoke*, a play with music, about the railway 'improvements' and clearances of 1863; *Boom*, a community play set in 1936, about the housing boom in the South East; *Extensions of Love*, about one woman's obsession with another and *Worlds Apart*, set in India and the UK. Adaptations for children have included *The Snow Queen, The Little Mermaid, 1001 Arabian Nights* and *Clara and the Nutcracker.* Short plays include *The Gallery,* and the ten minute musical *Dying for a Kipp* at Greenwich Theatre. In 2007 he wrote and co-directed *Payback* for Greenwich and Lewisham Young Peoples' Theatre and *Departures* for the National Youth Theatre. He has written and directed two short films *It Is* and *The Race,* is a writer on *Doctors* for the BBC and has two feature films in development. Darren has been short listed for the Carl Forman Award at BAFTA, is a selected short film writer for TAPS and was a finalists in the BBC Talent Television Drama initiative in 2002. His radio play *Vital Statistics* was part of BBC Radio Drama/Hampstead Theatre's 'Stages of Sound' 2006.

   Darren is also Artistic Director of *Spanner in the Works,* who run drama based workshops in schools, hospitals and museums and a freelance drama trainer and facilitator.

www.ingramcontent.com/pod-product-compliance
Lightning Source LLC
Chambersburg PA
CBHW072232190626
46809CB00017B/1858